MW00952983

We Are Penn State!

Sue and Joe Paterno

Illustrated by Justin Hilton

www.mascotbooks.com

It was Homecoming at Penn State. Fans and alumni traveled back to Happy Valley for a fun weekend of Penn State celebrations.

Penn State's proud mascot, the Nittany Lion, marched in the Homecoming Parade. Penn State fans cheered, "We are Penn State!"

After the parade, it was time for the
Homecoming Pep Rally at Old Main.
The Lion led Penn State cheers.

Coach Paterno and the Penn State football
team took the stage. Coach Paterno cheered,
"We are Penn State!"

The Lion stopped at the Nittany Lion Shrine,
where he ran into Mrs. Paterno. It was time to
"Guard the Shrine" - a homecoming tradition
at Penn State.

The Lion, Mrs. Paterno, and Penn State
students carefully watched over the Shrine.
Mrs. Paterno cheered,
"We are Penn State!"

The next afternoon, the Lion joined many
families at the Creamery. The Lion
ordered a scoop of "Peachy Paterno."

Families were enjoying the beautiful day
and the delicious ice cream.
Everyone cheered, "We are Penn State!"

The Lion joined his friends at Penn State
parties around Beaver Stadium.

Campers filled with Penn State fans arrived for the big game. As fans arrived at the stadium, they cheered, "We are Penn State!"

The Lion joined the football team in the locker room. Coach Paterno was giving the team final instructions. He told the young men to play hard and with good sportsmanship.

Ready for the game to begin, the football
team raised their arms and cheered,
"We are Penn State!"

Before the game, the Blue Band took
the field. The Drum Major ran onto the
field and landed a perfect flip!

The Blue Band then moved into formation.
Penn State fans cheered,
"We are Penn State!"

Led by Coach Paterno, the football team
took the field. They were greeted by
over 100,000 loyal Penn State fans.

The team ran out of the tunnel
cheering, "We are Penn State!"

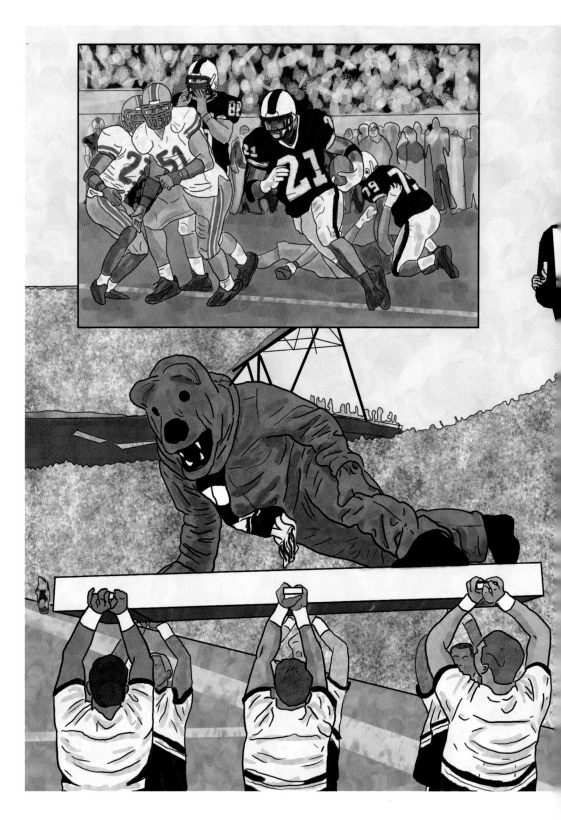

The Penn State football team played like champions. After every score, a lion's roar could be heard in the stadium.

The Nittany Lion did push-ups after every touchdown. The cheerleaders cheered, "We are Penn State!"

The Lion joined his friends in the student
section. The students showed their spirit
by dressing in blue and white.

The students lifted the Lion high into the air and
passed him all around. As they lifted the Lion,
they cheered, "We are Penn State!"

Penn State won the football game.
Players, coaches, and fans celebrated
the Homecoming game victory.

As the football team left the field,
fans cheered, "We are Penn State!"

To all Penn State fans. Thank you for making
Penn State the magical place that we hold so
close to our hearts. ~ Sue and Joe Paterno

For my wife Patricia. Thank you for all your support. ~ Justin Hilton

For more information about our products,
please visit us online at www.mascotbooks.com.

For more information, please contact Mascot Books,
P.O. Box 220157, Chantilly, VA 20153-0157

ISBN: 978-1-932888-49-2

Printed in the United States.

www.mascotbooks.com

Title List

Team	Book Title	Author
Baseball		
Boston Red Sox	Hello, Wally!	Jerry Remy
Boston Red Sox	Wally And His Journey Through Red Sox Nation!	Jerry Remy
New York Yankees	Let's Go, Yankees!	Yogi Berra
New York Mets	Hello, Mr. Met!	Rusty Staub
St. Louis Cardinals	Hello, Fredbird!	Ozzie Smith
Philadelphia Phillies	Hello, Phillie Phanatic!	Aimee Aryal
Chicago Cubs	Let's Go, Cubs!	Aimee Aryal
Chicago White Sox	Let's Go, White Sox!	Aimee Aryal
Cleveland Indians	Hello, Slider!	Bob Feller

Team	Book Title	Author
Pro Football		
Carolina Panthers	Let's Go, Panthers!	Aimee Aryal
Dallas Cowboys	How 'Bout Them Cowboys!	Aimee Aryal
Green Bay Packers	Go, Packres, Go!	Aimee Aryal
Kansas City Chiefs	Let's Go, Chiefs!	Aimee Aryal
Minnesota Vikings	Let's Go, Vikings!	Aimee Aryal
New York Giants	Let's Go, Giants!	Aimee Aryal
New England Patriots	Let's Go, Patriots!	Aimee Aryal
Seattle Seahawks	Let's Go, Seahawks!	Aimee Aryal
Washington Redskins	Hail To The Redskins!	Aimee Aryal
Coloring Book		
Dallas Cowboys	How 'Bout Them Cowboys!	Aimee Aryal

Team	Book Title	Author
College		
Alabama	Hello, Big Al!	Aimee Aryal
Alabama	Roll Tide!	Ken Stabler
Arizona	Hello, Wilbur!	Lute Olsen
Arkansas	Hello, Big Red!	Aimee Aryal
Auburn	Hello, Aubie!	Aimee Aryal
Auburn	War Eagle!	Pat Dye
Boston College	Hello, Baldwin!	Aimee Aryal
Brigham Young	Hello, Cosmo!	LaVell Edwards
Clemson	Hello, Tiger!	Aimee Aryal
Colorado	Hello, Ralphie!	Aimee Aryal
Connecticut	Hello, Jonathan!	Aimee Aryal
Duke	Hello, Blue Devil!	Aimee Aryal
Florida	Hello, Albert!	Aimee Aryal
Florida State	Let's Go, 'Noles!	Aimee Aryal
Georgia	Hello, Hairy Dawg!	Aimee Aryal
Georgia	How 'Bout Them Dawgs!	Vince Dooley
Georgia Tech	Hello, Buzz!	Aimee Aryal
Illinois	Let's Go, Illini!	Aimee Aryal
Indiana	Let's Go, Hoosiers!	Aimee Aryal
Iowa	Hello, Herky!	Aimee Aryal
Iowa State	Hello, Cy!	Amy DeLashmutt
James Madison	Hello, Duke Dog!	Aimee Aryal
Kansas	Hello, Big Jay!	Aimee Aryal
Kansas State	Hello, Willie!	Dan Walter
Kentucky	Hello, Wildcat!	Aimee Aryal
Louisiana State	Hello, Mike!	Aimee Aryal
Maryland	Hello, Testudo!	Aimee Aryal
Michigan	Let's Go, Blue!	Aimee Aryal

Team	Book Title	Author
Michigan State	Hello, Sparty!	Aimee Aryal
Minnesota	Hello, Goldy!	Aimee Aryal
Mississippi	Hello, Colonel Rebel!	Aimee Aryal
Mississippi State	Hello, Bully!	Aimee Aryal
Missouri	Hello, Truman!	Todd Donoho
Nebraska	Hello, Herbie Husker!	Aimee Aryal
North Carolina	Hello, Rameses!	Aimee Aryal
North Carolina St.	Hello, Mr. Wuf!	Aimee Aryal
Notre Dame	Let's Go, Irish!	Aimee Aryal
Ohio State	Hello, Brutus!	Aimee Aryal
Oklahoma	Let's Go, Sooners!	Aimee Aryal
Oklahoma State	Hello, Pistol Pete!	Aimee Aryal
Penn State	Hello, Nittany Lion!	Aimee Aryal
Penn State	We Are Penn State!	Joe Paterno
Purdue	Hello, Purdue Pete!	Aimee Aryal
Rutgers	Hello, Scarlet Knight!	Aimee Aryal
South Carolina	Hello, Cocky!	Aimee Aryal
So. California	Hello, Tommy Trojan!	Aimee Aryal
Syracuse	Hello, Otto!	Aimee Aryal
Tennessee	Hello, Smokey!	Aimee Aryal
Texas	Hello, Hook 'Em!	Aimee Aryal
Texas A & M	Howdy, Reveille!	Aimee Aryal
UCLA	Hello, Joe Bruin!	Aimee Aryal
Virginia	Hello, CavMan!	Aimee Aryal
Virginia Tech	Hello, Hokie Bird!	Aimee Aryal
Virginia Tech	Yea, It's Hokie Game Day!	Frank Beamer
Wake Forest	Hello, Demon Deacon!	Aimee Aryal
West Virginia	Hello, Mountaineer!	Aimee Aryal
Wisconsin	Hello, Bucky!	Aimee Aryal

Team	Book Title	Author
NBA		
Dallas Mavericks	Let's Go, Mavs!	Mark Cuban
Kentucky Derby		
Kentucky Derby	White Diamond Runs For The Roses	Aimee Aryal

More great titles coming soon!

info@mascotbooks.com